The Fairies'
Birthday Surprise

The Rainbow Fairies

Amber the Orange Fairy

Sky the Blue Fairy

Fern the Green Fairy

Heather the Violet Fairy

Sunny the Yellow Fairy

Ruby the Red Fairy

Inky the Indigo Fairy

Library of Congress Cataloging-in-Publication Data is available.

ISBN 978-0-545-22292-1

10 9 8 7 6 5 4 3 2 1   10 11 12 13/0

Printed in the U.S.A.   40
First printing, August 2010

The Fairies'
Birthday Surprise

By Daisy Meadows

SCHOLASTIC INC.

New York   Toronto   London   Auckland

Sydney   Mexico City   New Delhi   Hong Kong

A trumpet sounds from Fairyland castle, and the Rainbow Fairies awake.

"Is that the royal trumpet?" Ruby asks.
"Yes, today is the Fairy Queen's
birthday!" Sky remembers.
"We should do something special for her,"
Fern says.

"Let's bake her a cake," Inky says.

"Yes," Sunny agrees. "Let's make it from scratch."

"What does that mean?" Heather asks.

"It means we'll make it by hand," Sunny
explains, "and we won't use magic."
The fairy sisters look at one another.
They *always* use magic.

"Making it from scratch is special," Ruby
says. "Let's do it!"

Amber opens a cookbook.

"The recipe calls for sugar, butter, eggs, flour,
baking powder, and milk," she reads aloud.

"We don't have eggs, milk, or butter," she
says, looking up.

"I can make them!" Heather suggests, raising her wand.

"Wait!" declares Sunny. "We all agreed, no [...]c."

The Rainbow Fairies fly to the Fairyland farm. Ruby, Amber, and Inky head into the henhouse.

"Cluckity cluck," the hens call as the
fairies take eggs from their warm nests.
"Thank you, ladies," Inky says as they leave.

The other fairies are in the cow barn.
"The recipe calls for milk and butter,"
remembers Fern.

"We can churn the milk into butter,"
Heather says.
Sunny and Sky sit down on the stools and
begin to milk.

The fairies put the eggs and milk in a wagon, and Sunny pulls it.

"This is hard work!" she says.

"It would be easier with magic," says Heather.

"But we agreed," Inky insists.

"I know," answers Heather, "no magic."

The fairies return to the cottage.

Ruby and Amber crack the eggs.

Sunny and Fern churn the butter.
Sky, Inky, and Heather mix the batter.
It is messy work!

The fairies pour the batter into seven pans and put them in the oven.

Amber looks at the clock. "The cakes should
be done just in time for the party," she says.
"We'll clean up while they bake," says Sunny.

Ding!

"They are ready!" Fern declares.

Each fairy pulls a cake from the oven.

They stack the seven cakes and admire their hard work.

"Oh, no!" cries Sunny. "We forgot the icing."

"We don't have time to make icing from
scratch," Amber says.
"We worked so hard," Ruby says. "A little
magic couldn't hurt."

Sparkles whirl from Ruby's wand and swirl around the cake.

At once, the cake is covered with white icing!

"Now we need to add color," says Ruby.

But the fairies cannot agree on how to
decorate the cake.

Fern says, "The bottom layer should be green,
like grass." She flicks her wand, and green
icing covers the bottom cake.

"No, it should be blue," insists Sky.

All of the fairies want to make the cake
pretty, and each fairy has her own favorite
color.
They all point their wands at the cake at the
same time.
Whoosh! Sparkles spin around the kitchen.

"What's happening?" asks Sky. "The sparkles won't stop."

"Maybe we used too much magic," Inky suggests.

When the sparkles disappear, the fairies
gasp.
The cake is a mess of color.

"What should we do?" Sunny asks. "The party is starting."

"I don't think we should use any more magic," Amber says.

"We baked a cake for the queen," says Inky. "We should give it to her."

The fairy sisters put the cake in their wagon
and pull it to the royal garden.
The party has started, but the crowd grows
quiet as the Rainbow Fairies wheel in
the cake.
The king and queen stand.

"You baked me a cake!" says the Fairy Queen.
Amber cuts a piece and hands it to the queen.

The queen takes a bite. "It's delicious!" she exclaims. "It reminds me of my birthday cakes as a little fairy. My mother and I made them from scratch." She takes another bite.

"Except for the icing. We used a little magic for that." The queen smiles at the sisters. "I love the colorful icing. Only the Rainbow Fairies could have made this cake! It's a real treat."

When they are done serving the guests, the Rainbow Fairies sit down to have some cake, too. "It's wonderful," says Amber.

"It is good," Heather agrees, "but my piece needs more icing." She gives her wand a twirl and a big frosted flower appears. "Yum!" she exclaims. "Now it tastes magical!"